Dream It, Do It!

GET DRAWING!

Charlotte Guillain

Heinemann
LIBRARY

Chicago, Illinois

Huntington City
Township Public Library
255 West Park Drive
Huntington, IN 46750

Edited by Rebecca Rissman, Dan Nunn, and Helen Cox Cannons
Designed by Steve Mead
Original illustrations © Capstone Global Library, Ltd
Picture research by Ruth Blair
Production by Vicki Fitzgerald
Originated by Capstone Global Library, Ltd
Printed and bound in China by CTPS

17 16 15 14 13
10 9 8 7 6 5 4 3 2 1

Library of Congress Cataloging-in-Publication Data
Guillain, Charlotte.
  Get drawing! / Charlotte Guillain.
      pages cm.—(Dream it, do it!)
Includes bibliographical references and index.
ISBN 978-1-4109-6262-1 (hb)—ISBN 978-1-4109-6267-6 (pb) 1. Drawing—
Technique. 2. Art—Vocational guidance. I. Title.

NC730.G85 2014
741.2—dc23   2013017422

Acknowledgments
The author and publisher are grateful to the following for permission
to reproduce copyright material: Alamy pp. 13 (© Anthony Hatley),
21 (© Photo Art Collection (PAC)); Capstone Publishers pp. 15 top &
bottom, 16, 17, 26, 27, 28, 29 (all © Karon Dubke), 19 (Steve Walker/
Dawn Beacon/Stella Plage); Getty Images pp. 9 (Jupiterimages),
24 (Fotos International), 25 (Trish Gant); iStockphoto p. 23 (© Gabor
Izso); Shutterstock pp. 5 (© Artush), 7 left (© ETIENjones), 7 right (©
oksana2010), 11 (© sevenke), 12 (© Tenki), 19. Incidental photographs
reproduced with permission of: graph paper, Shutterstock (© optimarc);
felt tip pens, Shutterstock (© nikkytok); watercolor paper, Shutterstock
(© Aleksandr Stennikov).

Cover photograph of children drawing into the air reproduced with
permission of Getty Images (MECKY).

We would like to thank Adam Guillain for his invaluable help in the
preparation of this book.

CONTENTS

Some words are shown in bold, **like this**. You can find out what they mean by looking in the glossary.

BE AN ARTIST!

Have you always wanted to be an artist? Have you dreamed of drawing wonderful pictures but don't know where to start? This book will help you make your dreams come true.

Read on and find out how to stop dreaming and get drawing!

WHAT DO YOU NEED?

Gather together any of these **materials** that you might need to get drawing:

Drawing pencils
Colored pencils
Drawing pens
Chalk
Charcoal
White and colored paper
Textured paper
Squared paper
Scrapbook
Sketchbook

Collect all the things you need in one place. Try to use something new each time you draw.

FINDING INSPIRATION

Ideas come when you don't expect them. Carry a sketchpad with you and keep all your drawings and doodles. You could also cut out any pictures that you like in magazines and stick them in your sketchpad.

Inspiration

Decorate the cover of your sketchpad with photos and pictures that inspire you.

PLAYING WITH PENCIL AND PAPER

It's a good idea to warm up when you start drawing. Try taking a line for a walk on a piece of paper and see where it takes you! Practice drawing circles and see how perfect you can make them, or see what they turn into.

Activity

Draw a squiggle for a friend, and then get your friend to finish the squiggle to make a complete drawing. Then swap!

SHAPES

Look for the big shapes in the objects that you try to draw. Sketch these shapes lightly first, and then start to fill in the details.

Activity

Look carefully in a mirror and see what shapes make up your face. Try to draw a **self-portrait**, starting with the shape of your head and then looking at where your eyes, nose, and mouth sit.

LIGHT AND SHADOW

Light is very important when you're drawing. Experiment by shining a light from different sides and angles on an object that you want to draw. How do the shapes and shadows that you can see change?

Activity

Try using lines and dots to fill in your drawings. Cross the lines or draw the dots closer together in the dark parts, and space them out more in the lighter areas.

DRAWING PEOPLE

Look at people around you and in pictures. How do the different parts of their bodies fit together? How far down their body do their arms reach? What do they look like from the side? Look at how other artists have drawn people.

Activity

1. Stick a sheet of colored paper on the wall.
2. Get a friend to stand next to the paper. Get someone else to shine a flashlight toward your friend.
3. Draw around the shadow of your friend's head on the piece of paper. Then cut it out.
4. You now have a **silhouette** of your friend's head!

ILLUSTRATING STORIES

If you are stuck for ideas of what to draw, try drawing **illustrations** for your favorite books. Think about the characters before you start—how will you show their personalities? If the book already has pictures, try to choose a section that doesn't have illustrations.

Inspiration

Look at other illustrators' drawings. Whose style do you like? Try copying their drawings and develop your own style using theirs as a starting point.

GET COLORFUL

You can enjoy experimenting with color when you draw. Look carefully at the colors of things that you draw. How do they change in light and shadow? You can use unusual colors to show different feelings and moods.

Activity

Draw a picture of yourself looking happy, and a picture where you look sad or angry. Which colors could you use to show your different feelings?

What do the colors in this painting tell you about how the girl is feeling?

LOOK DIFFERENTLY

When you're drawing, it is interesting to look at the world around you in new and different ways. Try drawing things from different viewpoints, for example, looking down from above or up from below. Or you could try drawing things upside down!

Activity

Choose one section of the thing you want to draw. Zoom in so you draw that part **magnified** very close up.

23

DRAWING CARTOONS

Do you like reading comics or watching cartoons? Try drawing your own cartoons. Look at how the **illustrations** in comics show people and objects in a different way from other artists. Practice copying their styles, and then make your own comic strip telling a short story or joke.

Activity

In a small notebook, draw a cartoon character on the first page. On each page that follows, draw the same character but move him or her slightly each time. When you've finished, flick the pages of the book and watch your character move!

SET UP A GALLERY

All artists need to share their work!
Put your drawings in a gallery.

1. Choose your best drawings. Don't show
    too many—just choose the pictures
    that you are especially proud of. Try to
    show a range of pictures that use pencil,
    pen, crayon, chalk, and different types
    of paper. Can you show drawings in
    different styles?

2. You want your drawings to look good hanging on the wall. **Mount** each picture by sticking it onto colored paper that is slightly larger.

3. Write some information about each picture. How did you get the idea to draw it, and what materials did you use? Stick this information onto the corner of each mount.

4. Either stick your drawings on a blank wall or lay them out on a table.

5. Make a **catalog** for the people who are going to visit your gallery. This could be a leaflet with some information about you and how you got into drawing. Then list all the drawings that you're displaying in your gallery.

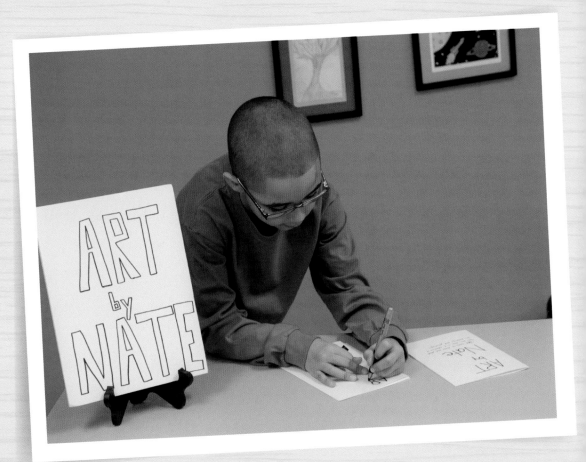

6. Invite your friends and family to a **private view**. Offer them a drink and some snacks, and talk to them about your drawings. They might have a lot of questions for you!

7. Make sure you take a lot of photos of your gallery for your scrapbook.

8. Start thinking of ideas for your next drawings!

GLOSSARY

catalog complete list of items

charcoal stick of burned wood or other matter used for drawing

illustration drawing or painting that shows events or characters in a story

magnified something that has been made to look larger than it really is

materials things needed for an activity

mount fix into position to display

private view special viewing of art in a gallery to which people are invited

self-portrait picture of yourself

silhouette outline of something dark against a light background

textured having a surface that has a pattern or bumps on it

FIND OUT MORE

Books

Hosack, Karen. *Drawings and Cartoons.* Chicago: Raintree, 2009.

McCurry, Kristen. *Smithsonian Drawing Books* (series). Mankato, Minn.: Capstone, 2013.

Web sites

FactHound offers a safe, fun way to find Internet sites related to this book. All of the sites on FactHound have been researched by our staff.

Here's all you do:

Visit www.facthound.com

Type in this code: 9781410962621

INDEX